The Deadly
Race to Space:
RUSSIA

BOOK (9)

Join Secret Agent Jack Stalwart on his other adventures:

**The Escape of the
Deadly Dinosaur:**
USA
Book ①

**The Search for the
Sunken Treasure:**
AUSTRALIA
Book ②

**The Mystery of
the Mona Lisa:**
FRANCE
Book ③

**The Caper of the
Crown Jewels:**
ENGLAND
Book ④

**The Secret of the
Sacred Temple:**
CAMBODIA
Book ⑤

**The Pursuit of the
Ivory Poachers:**
KENYA
Book ⑥

**The Puzzle of the
Missing Panda:**
CHINA
Book ⑦

**Peril at the
Grand Prix:**
ITALY
Book ⑧

**The Quest for
Aztec Gold:**
MEXICO
Book ⑩

The Deadly
Race to Space:
RUSSIA

Elizabeth Singer Hunt

Illustrated by Brian Williamson

WEINSTEIN BOOKS

ISBN: 978-1-60286-078-0

First Edition
10   9

For GG, who now sleeps with the stars

Destination:
RUSSIA

My name is Jack Stalwart. My older brother,

Max, was a secret agent for you, until he

disappeared on one of your missions. Now I

want to be a secret agent too. If you choose

me, I will be an excellent secret agent and get

rid of evil villains, just like my brother did.

Sincerely,

Jack Stalwart

HIGHLY CONFIDENTIAL

Jack Stalwart was sworn in as a Global Protection Force secret agent four months ago. Since that time, he has completed all of his missions successfully and has stopped no less than twelve evil villains. Because of this he has been assigned the code name "COURAGE".

Jack has yet to uncover the whereabouts of his brother, Max, who is still working for this organization at a secret location. Do not give Secret Agent Jack Stalwart this information. He is never to know about his brother.

Gerald Barter
Director, Global Protection Force

THINGS YOU'LL FIND IN EVERY BOOK

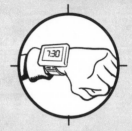

Watch Phone: The only gadget Jack wears all the time, even when he's not on official business. His Watch Phone is the central gadget that makes most others work. There are lots of important features, most importantly the "C" button, which reveals the code of the day—necessary to unlock Jack's Secret Agent Book Bag. There are buttons on both sides, one of which ejects his life-saving Melting Ink Pen. Beyond these functions, it also works as a phone and, of course, gives Jack the time of day.

Global Protection Force (GPF): The GPF is the organization Jack works for. It's a worldwide force of young secret agents whose aim is to protect the world's people, places and possessions. No one knows exactly where its main offices are located (all correspondence and gadgets for repair are sent to a special PO Box, and training is held at various locations around the world), but Jack thinks it's somewhere cold, like the Arctic Circle.

Whizzy: Jack's magical miniature globe. Almost every night at precisely 7:30 P.M., the GPF uses Whizzy to send Jack the identity of the country that he must travel to. Whizzy can't talk, but he can cough up messages. Jack's parents don't know Whizzy is anything more than a normal globe.

The Magic Map: The magical map hanging on Jack's bedroom wall. Unlike most maps, the GPF's map is made of a mysterious wood. Once Jack inserts the country piece from Whizzy, the map swallows Jack whole and sends him away on his missions. When he returns, he arrives precisely one minute after he left.

Secret Agent Book Bag: The Book Bag that Jack wears on every adventure. Licensed only to GPF secret agents, it contains top-secret gadgets necessary to foil bad guys and escape certain death. To activate the bag before each mission, Jack must punch in a secret code given to him by his Watch Phone. Once he's away, all he has to do is place his finger on the zip, which identifies him as the owner of the bag and immediately opens.

THE STALWART FAMILY

Jack's dad, John

He moved the family to England when Jack was two, in order to take a job with an aerospace company. Jack's dad thinks he is an ordinary boy and that his other son, Max, attends a school in Switzerland. Jack's dad is American and his mum is British, which makes Jack a bit of both.

Jack's mum, Corinne

One of the greatest mums as far as Jack is concerned. When she and her husband received a letter from a posh school in Switzerland inviting Max to attend, they were overjoyed. Since Max left six months ago, they have received numerous notes in Max's handwriting telling them he's OK. Little do they know it's all a lie and that it's the GPF sending those letters.

Jack's older brother, Max

Two years ago, at the age of nine, Max joined the GPF. Max used to tell Jack about his adventures and show him how to work his secret-agent gadgets. When the family received a letter inviting Max to attend a school in Europe, Jack figured it was to do with the GPF. Max told him he was right, but that he couldn't tell Jack anything about why he was going away.

Nine-year-old Jack Stalwart

Four months ago, Jack received an anonymous note saying: "Your brother is in danger. Only you can save him." As soon as he could, Jack applied to be a secret agent too. Since that time, he's battled some of the world's most dangerous villains, and hopes some day in his travels to find and rescue his brother, Max.

DESTINATION:

Russia

The main language of Russia is Russian. It is based on a 33-letter alphabet called the Cyrillic alphabet.

□

Russia's currency is the Ruble.

□

The first man in space was a Russian named Yuri Gagarin. Today Russia operates the world's oldest and largest space launch facility, the Baikonur Cosmodrome.

Russia is the largest country on the planet. It stretches from northeast Europe across to northern Asia.

□

Its proper name is the Russian Federation.

□

Moscow is Russia's capital city and the largest city in Europe. 11 million people live there.

SPACE CRAFTS: FACTS AND FIGURES

In 1957, the Russians sent the first ever space craft, called *Sputnik 1*, into space.

Space rockets are usually made of several sections. The bottom sections carry the fuel and the top sections carry the astronauts.

When the bottom sections of fuel are used up, they usually fall off. Kerosene and liquid hydrogen are typically used to fuel the rocket.

A rocket needs to travel at 25,250 miles per hour (40,635 km/h) to escape Earth's gravity and at least 17,500 mph (28,165 km/h) to keep it circling around Earth.

THE SOLAR SYSTEM

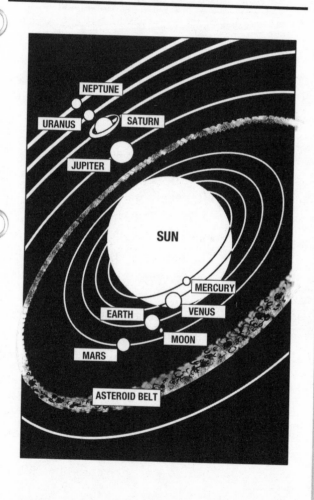

MARS: FACTS AND FIGURES

Mars is called the "red planet." It got its name from the Romans, who named it after the god of war. (Red reminded them of blood).

It's the closest planet to Earth in the Solar System— only 300 million miles (480 million km) away.

The surface of Mars is dry and dusty, with lots of rocks and craters. One of the largest craters is 200 miles (320 km) across and thousands of miles long.

Mars has a North and South Pole that are covered by ice and frozen carbon dioxide. Temperatures at the poles can drop to as low as −115°C.

Mars used to have running water. Scientists have seen pictures that show riverbeds and flat areas that could have been oceans.

Gravity on Mars is only ⅓ of Earth's. If you weighed 40 kilograms (90 pounds) on Earth, you'd only weigh 13.34 kilograms (30 pounds) on Mars.

RUSSIAN ALPHABET

А а (A)	**Р р** (R)
Б б (B)	**С с** (S)
В в (V)	**Т т** (T)
Г г (G)	**У у** (U)
Д д (D)	**Ф ф** (F)
Е е (E)	**Х х** (KH)
Ё ё (YO)	**Ц ц** (TS)
Ж ж (ZH)	**Ч ч** (CH)
З з (Z)	**Ш ш** (SH)
И и (I)	**Щ щ** (SHCH)
Й й (Y)	**ъ** (–)
К к (K)	**ы** (Y)
Л л (L)	**ь** (')
М м (M)	**Э э** (E)
Н н (N)	**Ю ю** (YU or IU)
О о (O)	**Я я** (YA or IA)
П п (P)	

SECRET AGENT GADGET INSTRUCTION MANUAL

Smoke-Screen Pellets: When you need to distract someone or something, use the GPF's Smoke-Screen Pellets. These sticky blue pellets emit smoke so thick it's impossible to see anything through it for two minutes. Just throw them at your target—they activate on impact.

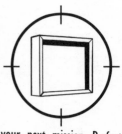

Portable Map: Small enough to fit in your Book Bag, this wooden square opens up to the size of your Magic Map. Just place the jigsaw piece inside as normal and it will transport you to your next mission. Perfect when you're traveling and away from home.

Mind Eraser: When you
need to erase somebody's short-term memory, hand them the GPF's Mind Eraser. Just flick the switch on this rectangular box and tell them to stare at the swirling spirals inside. After a few minutes, they'll forget what happened in the last 48 hours.

Gripper Gloves: If you
need a little extra grip, slip on a pair of Gripper Gloves. These gloves have a special grip fabric that prevents you from slipping, even on the smoothest of materials. Great for climbing shiny poles, steel columns or any outdoor structure.

Chapter 1:
The Night Sky

It was a clear, dark night, and Jack
Stalwart was lying on his back gazing at
the stars. He was with his local Scouts
group on a camping trip in the New Forest
in England. As part of the activities, his
troop leader had told Jack and the other
boys to observe the night sky, try to spot
the constellations and think about the
possibility of life beyond planet Earth.

1

"Do you see that star over there?" asked Jack's friend Richard, pointing to a brilliant white light. "It's not a star," he said, "but the International Space Station—the brightest light in the night sky."

Jack knew that Richard was right. The International Space Station—also known as the ISS—was a man-made satellite that orbited 220 miles, or 354 kilometers, above Earth. It was the biggest laboratory in the sky, where scientists carried out research on everything from cancer to how plants grow and the effects of living in space.

Astronauts were constantly being ferried to and from the ISS. It took them about two days to get there. Once they were there, they could stay for months, and the longest any astronaut had lived on the station was two years. Jack knew a lot about the ISS because the GPF received daily "live" updates.

The GPF, or Global Protection Force, was the organization that Jack worked for. He was a secret agent for them, traveling the globe to protect the world's most precious treasures. But no one knew anything about that—not even his family or his best friends.

Richard and Jack continued staring at all the stars. Their other friend, Charlie, was lying beside them, making a note of the constellations they could see, like Orion.

"I can't believe we're finally going to send a human to Mars," said Jack. He stretched out his arms, placed his hands behind his head and thought about how amazing it was.

Tomorrow's Mars mission was all over the news. After decades of planning, a team of Americans and Russians were sending six astronauts—three men and three women—to the red planet.

It would take more than a year to complete the journey, but it didn't matter how long it took. Sending a human to Mars was one of the biggest things in space history—as important as when the American astronaut Neil Armstrong walked on the moon.

"I know," said Charlie. "It's incredible. I wonder what the astronauts are doing right now."

"Did you know," said Jack, "that my dad's going to be there? He's going to see the rocket liftoff up close." Jack couldn't help but brag about his dad, who was an aerospace engineer. During his career, he'd helped design some American spy

satellites, and parts of the International Space Station.

Since moving to England, Jack's father only worked on special projects. A few years ago he'd been awarded the job of designing the Mars spacecraft itself. He was in Russia right now, supervising the final details before the rocket was launched.

"That's what I want to be when I'm older," said Charlie.

"An aerospace engineer?" asked Jack, still thinking about his dad.

"No, you silly," said Charlie. "An astronaut!"

"You—an astronaut?" said Richard, teasing Charlie. "You don't have what it takes!"

"Yes, I do," said Charlie. "You watch," he told them. "I'm going to be the first person to walk on Jupiter!"

Jack and Richard looked at each other and then cracked up laughing. There was no way Charlie was going to "walk" on Jupiter. Except for a tiny rock core, Jupiter was nothing but a big ball of gas.

Chapter 2:
The Portable Map

As Jack lay there imagining Charlie in
space, he heard a small beep coming
from his GPF Watch Phone. It was 7:25 P.M.,
and he had to find somewhere secure.
It didn't matter that Jack was in the
middle of Scouts, he had to be ready to
respond.

Telling his friends he needed the "restroom," Jack wandered off and found a
hidden spot behind some trees in the

forest. Reaching into the front pocket of his Book Bag, he pulled out his miniature globe, named Whizzy.

"Hi, Whizzy," said Jack, placing the magic globe in the palm of his hand.

As the clock ticked over to 7:30 P.M., Whizzy winked and began to spin. The faster he got, the more he tickled Jack's hand, until he coughed—*ahem!*—and a giant jigsaw piece popped out of his mouth.

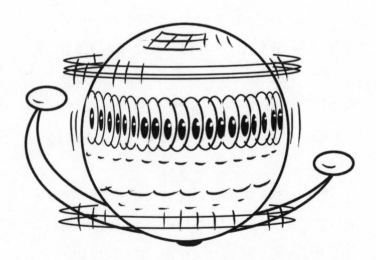

Normally, if Jack were at home, he'd slip the piece into the Magic Map, on his wall. Then he'd know the exact location of his next adventure. But for moments like this—when secret agents were away from home—the GPF had created another way to transport them to their destination.

Jack put a tired Whizzy back into the pocket of his Book Bag and keyed the letter "C" into his Watch Phone. The code word C-A-V-I-A-R appeared on the screen, and he tapped the letters into his Book Bag's lock.

As his Secret Agent Book Bag popped open, Jack looked around to make sure that no one was nearby. Inside his bag were some new gadgets: the Mind Eraser, the Noggin Mold and the SatMap device. But fitted into a side pocket was what he was looking for—a thin wooden board folded up on its hinges into a tidy square.

Jack unfolded the board until it grew to twice his size and showed a big map of the world. He laid it down on the ground, picked up the jigsaw piece and began to trace it over the map. The piece was so big it was easy to guess which country it would be. When Jack got to the top of Asia the jigsaw piece slipped in, and the name RUSSIA flashed before his eyes. Now Jack knew where he was headed, but as always, he didn't know why.

Maybe someone had stolen a priceless

Fabergé egg from a Moscow museum. Or perhaps the president of Russia was in trouble at the Kremlin. As the white light inside the country on his board began to glow, Jack stepped onto the wooden map and shut his eyes. Opening one eye quickly to make sure that no one was watching, he yelled, "Off to Russia!"

With those words and a burst of light, Jack and his portable Magic Map disappeared from the forest.

Chapter 3:
The Missing Man

As soon as Jack arrived in Russia, he
packed away his map and took a good
look around. He was at the back of a large
semicircular room filled with dozens of
people. Most were busy at work, seated
in front of computers. Others were talking
and walking around. From what Jack could
tell, they were speaking English, although
he could hear bits of Russian, French and
Italian too.

High on the wall and at the front was a giant movie screen. Every few seconds the image on the screen would change. The first was of some flatbed trucks carrying goods, and the next was of a cockpit with six seats inside. The last was of a tall, brown rocket. Suddenly Jack realized where he was, and he tried to duck out of view.

"Hello, there," said a husky voice, startling Jack.

Jack turned to his side. Standing beside him was a man wearing a gray jacket, white shirt and black tie.

"You must be Jack," he said, holding out his hand. Although he was speaking in English, the man sounded Russian.

Jack paused. He thought he recognized the man from somewhere.

"I'm Yuri," the man said. "Yuri Ivanov."

Now Jack knew who he was. Yuri was

the person in charge of the Mars mission launch. He was Jack's dad's boss.

Although Jack hadn't met him before, he'd seen pictures of Yuri in the *GPF News*—the electronic newspaper for everyone who worked for the GPF. The Mars project was so important that everyone was talking about it.

Yuri had a strong, square-shaped face. He was handsome except for the bushy white eyebrows that hung over his pale blue eyes.

"*Privet*," said Jack, respectfully shaking his hand. *Privet* was Russian for "hello." "It's a pleasure to meet you."

Yuri nodded back with a smile. Jack guessed he was pleased that he knew a bit of Russian.

"What seems to be the problem?" asked Jack, who was busily scanning the room for his dad. The last thing he needed was for his father to see him here.

"You see this?" Yuri asked, lifting his hands in the air. "This is the Mars Mission Control Center. The command center for the world's first manned mission to Mars."

"I know," said Jack. "Is there a problem with the launch?"

"Hopefully not, with your help," said Yuri. "In a few hours we are due to send the first humans to Mars. Everything is ready to go," he explained, "except for one thing."

"What's that?" asked Jack, who couldn't believe that something might be wrong.

Yuri took a deep breath. "One of our key engineers has disappeared."

Now, thought Jack, that's a problem. If something had gone wrong with one of the chief engineers, the launch to Mars would definitely be in trouble. As he listened to Yuri, he continued to look around for his dad.

Yuri carried on. "I need you to find this person and bring him back to Mission Control. Without him, we can't launch the rocket."

"Who's the missing person?" asked Jack, his eyes following a man who looked like his father from the back.

Yuri paused before answering. "John Stalwart," he said. As if Jack didn't know who that was, Yuri added, "The engineer who's vanished is your dad."

Chapter 4:
The Last Place

Jack shook his head, as if to get Yuri's voice out from between his ears. He couldn't believe what he was hearing.

"What do you mean?" he said. "My dad can't be missing. This is the biggest thing in his career. Maybe he's gone for a long walk or something."

"I don't think so," said Yuri. "He's been gone for quite a while."

"How long?" asked Jack, who was starting to worry.

"Since yesterday," replied Yuri.

Jack's thoughts traveled back to his home in England. The last time he and his mum had spoken to his dad was two days ago. He'd sounded excited about the project. There's no way he would just leave it behind.

"Why didn't you contact someone earlier?" asked Jack, getting annoyed that Yuri had left it so long.

"We didn't want to alarm anyone," said Yuri. "We thought that perhaps he'd taken himself off for a while—you know, to have a break. Working under conditions like this can be hard. But when he didn't come back this morning, we began to worry. That's when I decided to call the GPF."

Jack was getting nervous now. With at least one day gone, his dad could be anywhere. This wasn't good news.

"Do you think it's possible that someone took him?" asked Jack. He

didn't like to think about it, but there was
a possibility that his dad had been
kidnapped.

"Maybe," said Yuri. "We're competing
with several other space agencies," he
explained, "any one of which would
benefit from taking your dad. He knows
things that other engineers don't. After
all, he was the main designer of the Mars
spacecraft itself. Plus, he's the only one
with the code."

"What code?" asked Jack.

"The code that begins the countdown,"
said Yuri. "The ten-second countdown to
launch can only be activated by entering a
special code. And your dad," he added,
"is the only one who knows it."

Although Jack was worried about his
dad, he couldn't help but be impressed.
To be the only one with the code that
launched one of the biggest and most

famous space rockets in history was a pretty cool job.

"Where was he last seen?" asked Jack.

The Russian man pointed to a sign sticking up in the middle of the room. "He was sitting at his desk in the middle of Quadrant Three," said Yuri.

On the desk were letters that looked like a "T" and a "P" and a backward "N." *TPN* spells the word "three" in Russian.

Now that Jack had a starting point, he was anxious to get to work. He turned to Yuri. "Next time you see me, I'll have my dad," he promised.

"I hope so," said Yuri with a smile. "I'm counting on it."

Jack nodded a quick goodbye, and then dashed through the control center toward his dad's desk.

Chapter 5:
The Note

When Jack reached the desk, he recognized it immediately. In a big picture frame was a photo of the Stalwart family: Jack, Max and their parents. Jack remembered the day they took the photo. It was just before Max was shipped off to "school." He looked at his brother and thought about how much he missed him.

"I wish you were here," Jack said, closing his eyes and whispering to his

brother to bring him good luck. Then he put the picture back on the desk and began to look around for clues. There was no more time to lose.

Besides the family picture, his dad had some pencils, paper and rulers on his desk. As Jack looked through various things, he noticed a plain pad of paper to his right. On it was something scribbled in ink.

It said:

Maybe his dad's disappearance was related to this note, thought Jack. As he looked at the scribble, he realized there were four important clues.

Taking the Encryption Notebook from his Book Bag, Jack placed his thumb on the identification pad. When it recognized him as the owner, it switched itself on.

Looking at his Watch Phone, Jack noticed it was 5:30 A.M., Russian time. He grabbed his pen and began to take notes.

1) Not in Dad's handwriting.

2) Meeting place has three letters or words.

3) According to Yuri, he's been gone for at least one day.

4) Told to bring laptop.

Jack needed to work out who wrote this note. He pulled out his Signature ID, the only gadget in the world that could analyze someone's handwriting and tell an agent whose it was. As he scanned the device over the paper, the word CLASSIFIED popped up. Now, *that* was a surprise.

The GPF almost never classified someone's identity. Classified status was reserved for top-secret officials who the GPF believed were "free and clear" of bad behavior. Maybe whoever met Jack's dad had nothing to do with his disappearance after all.

Moving on to the next clue, Jack noticed that the location of the meeting was given as APH. Because he didn't know enough about the Mission Control complex, it was time to use the GPF's SatMap gadget.

The SatMap could display a 3-D map of any government building in the world, including its underground bunkers. It had this information thanks to pictures taken by agents on the ground and by satellites in space.

Jack typed in the related information. As the word LOADING appeared on the screen, he crossed his fingers and hoped it would provide the details he needed.

Within moments a virtual map of the Mars Mission Control Center grounds appeared on the SatMap. Jack used his finger to drag the cursor across the screen from one location to another, looking for any building with the letters APH.

There it was!

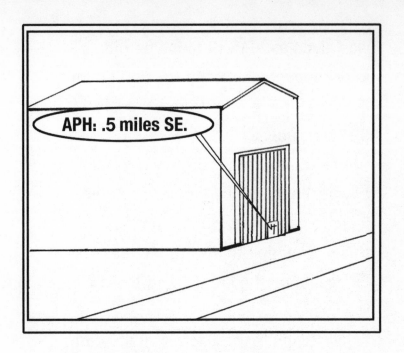

Jack tapped the screen, zooming in on the building. More information about the APH popped up.

Abandoned warehouse used for storage of faulty equipment.

That's odd, thought Jack. Why would Dad be meeting an important official in an abandoned warehouse?

Feeling uneasy, Jack locked his Book Bag and made his way toward the EXIT sign. Around him everyone was too busy at work to notice him. They didn't know that John Stalwart was missing, and that the launch they were working on was at risk.

According to the SatMap, the APH warehouse was half a mile southeast of the main building. Jack opened the doors to the outside and began to run. There was no time to waste. He had to find his dad.

Chapter 6:
The Brown Beauty

As Jack ran, he took a good look at the
grounds around Mission Control. It was
definitely a strange place. There were
barely any people outside and the ground
was dry and dusty. The only things around
were concrete buildings. If Jack hadn't
known they were making history inside,
he would have thought the whole place
was abandoned.

To his right and in the distance, Jack

spied a launchpad. He pulled his Google Goggles out of his Book Bag and flicked the switch to "maximum length". Within moments, he was gazing at the most beautiful rocket he'd ever seen. It was the Mars spacecraft itself—the very one his dad had designed. His father had shown him pictures of it before, but nothing compared to seeing it for real.

It was as tall as a skyscraper, and was painted a beautiful dark metallic brown. Russian and American flags decorated the middle, and at the top was a bright red triangular section. This was the "command module"—the cockpit where the astronauts would sit on their way into space.

Once the rocket had escaped from the Earth's gravitational pull, the command module would separate from the rest of the craft. It would take the astronauts to the ISS, where they would rest and then carry on for the orbit around Mars. Then, they would transfer to a Mars lander and make their long-awaited arrival on the red planet.

The plan was perfect, except for the fact that Jack's dad was missing and no one else knew the code to start the countdown.

Glancing back at the compass on his SatMap gadget, Jack made sure that it was pointing southeast. Then he started moving again. The APH was within reach, and hopefully, so was his dad.

Chapter 7:
The Attack

When Jack got to the building, he noticed
that it looked like an airplane hangar.
Makes sense, thought Jack, thinking of
the initials APH.

The hangar's roof was made of
corrugated iron, and the closed doors
were huge and on sliding rails. Jack put
the SatMap back into his bag as he
looked around for anyone or anything
suspicious.

Once he'd decided the outside was safe, Jack put his ear against the front doors of the building. He couldn't hear any noise inside, but just to be sure, he pulled out the GPF's Body-Count Tracker.

The Body-Count Tracker could map out walls and rooms and tell an agent if there were any people inside. It did this by showing a green or red dot. Green meant the person was alive and red meant they were dead.

According to the Body-Count Tracker, there was one steady green dot in the center of the building, and two moving green dots in the extreme left corner. Hoping that at least one of these dots was his dad, Jack carefully pulled the handle and the door slid open.

But as he stepped inside, a brilliant light flashed from the middle of the room and hit Jack's chest. It threw him

backward with such force that he fell and skidded on his backside.

As Jack lay there in the dirt, he wondered who and what had hit him. He'd heard about a criminal gadget that used the power of the sun to zap people. As he tried to pull himself up, his head started to spin. Jack had no energy. He slumped to the ground again.

The last thing Jack remembered was the sound of a man laughing and another coming toward him shouting the word "no." When he looked toward the voices, he thought he saw his dad.

"Dad," Jack called out to his father.

Then his eyes rolled backward and everything went black.

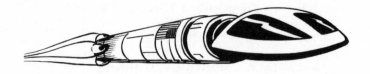

Chapter 8:
The Reason Why

When Jack came to, he was sitting in a chair with his head hanging down. His body was tired and rubbery, and a line of drool was hanging out of his mouth. He slurped it up, wiped his mouth on his shoulder, and tried to get control of his senses.

Jack didn't know how long he'd been unconscious, because he couldn't get to his Watch Phone. His wrists and chest were bound with tape behind his chair, and his feet were strapped up too. Although his Book Bag was still behind him, he couldn't reach any of his GPF gadgets, even his Melting Ink Pen.

Jack tried to remember the moment before he collapsed. What was that light that had hit him? Was that his dad running toward him? But where was he now? And who was responsible for tying Jack to the chair?

Suddenly he could hear voices. It was his dad! He was speaking to another man in a nearby room.

"Let him go," said his dad. "He's just a boy!"

"Is he?" the man replied. Jack recognized the thick Russian accent immediately. It was Yuri, and he wasn't being very nice. "Maybe you should ask him what he does in his spare time."

"What do you mean?" asked his dad. "He plays football! He does what any other ordinary boy does."

"That's what *you* think," sneered the Russian.

"What are you talking about?" asked John Stalwart.

Jack was getting worried. Was Yuri going to blow his cover? And why was he being so nasty?

"We're wasting time," said Yuri, moving on to something else. "You need to give me that launch code now."

"I told you before," said Jack's father. "I'm not going to give it to you. We need to add more water tanks and plastic shields to the rocket before I'll approve the liftoff."

Jack knew that one of the biggest dangers for astronauts flying outside of Earth's protective magnetic field was exposure to deadly galactic cosmic rays.

GCRs came from the sun and could penetrate even the thickest of metals.

They could get inside a spacecraft and damage human cells and organs, leading to death.

One of the best ways to protect the astronauts was by adding water tanks and hydrogen-based plastics to the inside walls of the spacecraft. Jack knew that his dad's original design included plenty of those, but it sounded as though he wanted to add more.

"What we have is fine!" shouted Yuri. "Adding additional tanks and plastics could take months!" he fumed. "I don't think I need to remind you that the Europeans are poised to launch their rocket too."

"I'm not giving you the code if lives are at risk," said Jack's dad. "And that's that."

"Perhaps I haven't made myself clear," said Yuri. His voice sounded evil now. "This is not for discussion. You will give me that code, or else."

"Or else what?" said John Stalwart angrily. Jack was proud that his dad didn't sound scared.

"Or else . . . your son will suffer because of you!" Yuri shouted.

Now Jack knew why he was here. He was "bait." Yuri was trying to use the threat of harming him to get to his dad. The GPF would be angry to hear that one of their agents had been called for and then used as a bargaining tool. Jack wondered if maybe this kind of trick had been used to lure and trap his missing brother, Max.

Everything went silent. There was a long pause in the conversation in the other room. Jack could almost feel his dad's anger through the walls before he suddenly let out a loud roar.

"You're not going to get away with this!" John Stalwart yelled. Jack could hear the sound of a fight. He really wanted to help his dad, but he couldn't move.

Yuri shouted something in Russian. Suddenly, the same flash of light that had hit Jack appeared from the other room.

Everything went quiet again. Then he heard a low moan. It sounded as though his dad had been zapped by the same thing.

"Westerners," he heard Yuri grunt. "We'll see *who* tells *who* what to do." Then he let out a sharp whistle. Jack heard more footsteps in the room. "Clean him up, Vigo," the Russian ordered. Then everything fell silent.

Chapter 9:
The Code

Jack sat there helplessly, trying to figure out what to do. He knew from his own experience that the light stunned rather than eliminated on impact. But he was still worried about his dad. Was he okay?

Jack heard some rustling, and then a man appeared at the door. He must be Vigo—the third green light on Jack's Body-Count Tracker and the guy Yuri had asked to "clean up" his dad.

Reaching behind him, Vigo pulled
something forward and then heaved it
across the floor. Jack eyes opened wide in
shock when he saw that it was his father.

Vigo left for a few moments and
reappeared with a chair. Placing it in front
of Jack, he lifted John Stalwart's body
onto it. Quickly, he taped his wrists and
feet, then strapped his chest to the chair
like Jack's. When he was finished, he
hurried off.

Jack took a look at his dad. Except for
having been knocked out, he looked fine—
no cuts or wounds.

"Uhhhh," groaned his dad. Jack could
see him struggle to open his eyes.

"Dad!" whispered Jack anxiously. "Are
you okay?"

"I'm okay," his dad replied. His speech
was slurred. "Are *you* okay?" he asked as
his head rolled from side to side. "What
was that light? I don't know how Yuri got

you here, but your mother must be very worried."

At the mention of his name, Yuri entered the room.

"How nice," he said with a wicked smile. "A family reunion—it warms the heart." Jack could tell from his voice that he wasn't being sincere.

"Shut it, Yuri," said Jack's dad, his eyes more focused now.

"Come now, John," said the Russian

with fake sympathy. "There's no need for that kind of reaction. Besides," he added, "you'll be happy to know that I may not need the two of you anyway."

Jack and his dad looked at Yuri.

"Remember that laptop you brought with you?" he asked, looking at Jack's dad. "Well, Alexei is about to extract the code."

Jack glanced at his dad. His normally rosy complexion was draining to a pale white.

"You see, Jack," Yuri explained, "a few days ago, your dad let slip that he'd hidden the code in a math puzzle on his computer. All I needed to do was lure him here, get his laptop, and then put my chief hacker, Alexei, on the job." The Russian man smiled to himself. "But just in case Alexei couldn't do it," he added, "I brought you here, to encourage your dad to cough up the code."

"You're mad!" screamed Jack's dad.
"You'll never get away with this. You need
my final approval for the launch anyway."

"You flatter yourself, John," said Yuri.
"That's what I'm *supposed* to do, but I'm
about to change the rules. After all, I'm
the boss. I'll just tell the others that in
the last few hours you've come down with
a bizarre illness, and I've isolated you in
the infirmary. With that little tidbit," Yuri
snickered, "no one will want to come
looking for you."

"You might be able to launch the rocket," said Jack's dad, "but as soon as I'm free, I'll tell the media! I'll see to it that the rocket is brought back down to Earth before any damage is done."

"You could do that, but you're assuming that I'm going to let you go," said Yuri. Then he let out an evil laugh.

Jack gulped. He knew what Yuri was planning to do . . . He was about to get rid of them both.

Just at that moment, Yuri received a phone call. He answered it in Russian. When he hung up, he smiled like a man who had just received the best news of his life.

"Alexei," he said, "has the code. That means you're not

needed anymore, John." Yuri motioned to his accomplice. "Vigo here," he explained, "is going to take you both for a ride. To a place where you'll be able to experience the power of the rocket firsthand."

As Yuri left the room, he added, "It will be the last thing either of you remembers."

Chapter 10:
The Deadly Drive

Vigo sliced through the tape around each of
their chests, and then loosened the rope
around their ankles only slightly. Yanking
them both to a standing position, he
shoved them out of the room and through
the main doors of the airplane hangar.

Once outside, Vigo directed them
toward a truck. Waddling toward it, the
Stalwarts looked like a couple of
penguins.

"If you let us go now," said Jack, trying
to reason with the Russian, "we promise
not to press charges."

Vigo laughed as he opened one of the
truck's doors.

"Get in!" he grunted. Jack guessed he
wasn't changing his mind.

Jack and his dad climbed awkwardly into the back. While Vigo got into the driver's seat, Jack quietly grabbed the door handle and tried to open it.

But it couldn't open from the inside. Vigo started the engine and drove off.

As they set off, Jack looked out of the window. There was no one in sight—nobody to signal to, or to cry to for help. He looked at his dad. Jack had never seen him look so worried.

Up ahead was the Mars spacecraft, which Vigo proceeded to drive around the back of. He pulled up alongside what looked like an electric fence and got out of the truck. He opened a padlock on the main gate and then drove through the entrance. As they passed by, Jack noticed a sign that read DANGER: RESTRICTED ACCESS ONLY.

Ignoring the warning, Vigo carried on until he found a secluded spot behind

some old scaffolding. There, he lugged
Jack and his dad out of the vehicle and
tossed them onto the tarmac. Jack could
hear his dad grunt in pain—he was still
feeling the shock from that burst of light.

Before Jack could do anything, Vigo reached down and tied their feet tightly together again. Satisfied that Jack and his dad were going nowhere fast, Vigo got back in the truck and started the engine. As he hit the accelerator, fumes from the exhaust blew into Jack's face. Coughing through the bad air, Jack watched Vigo drive in the direction of Mission Control.

From where he was lying, Jack could see the rocket's powerful boosters several hundred yards away. Knowing that any-thing within a mile of liftoff would be burned to a crisp, he closed his eyes and tried to think of a plan. The Stalwarts had to get out of there, and fast.

Chapter 11:
The Stalwart Idea

"Dad," said Jack, as soon as Vigo disappeared, "we have to get out of here!"

"I know," replied his dad, who was trying to sort through things in his head. "I'm working on that."

But Jack had already come up with an idea. "Look, Dad," he said, "I've got a plan. I need you to do exactly as I say."

"Wait a minute," said his dad, trying to calm Jack down. "I know you watch these ninja shows on TV. But watching them doesn't make you a ninja, okay? Stuff like this is better handled by a grown-up. You're still only nine, remember, Jack."

Jack almost wet himself laughing. If only his dad knew that he was an agent for the GPF.

"What's so funny?" asked his dad.

"Look, Dad," said Jack, "I know a few things. I can't tell you from where, but you have to trust me that I can get us free. Will you just listen to my idea at least?"

John Stalwart looked his son in the eye. "Okay," he said reluctantly. At least for the moment he seemed willing to listen.

Jack turned his back to his dad. "Right, roll over so that your back is facing mine." His dad did as he was told.

"Then try to reach the edge of the tape around my wrists," said Jack. He could feel his dad's fingers scraping along the tape, and finally he managed to grab a bit of the end.

"Now," Jack instructed, "try to peel it off." As John Stalwart pulled, Jack moved his hands up and down. As he did so, his dad was able to unravel the tape.

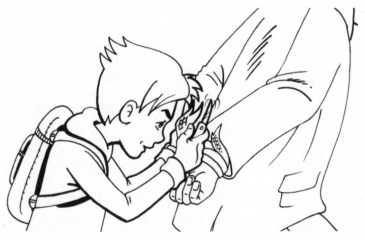

"Great!" said Jack, pushing himself into a sitting position. He reached into his Book Bag and took out his pocket knife.

Slicing through the tape around his feet, Jack was able to stand up. Rushing over to his dad, he did the same for him, cutting the tape from his hands and legs.

Jack's father looked impressed. "Well," he said, rubbing his wrists and ankles, "they've certainly taught you a few things in the Scouts!"

"Huh?" replied Jack, almost forgetting his dad didn't know about the GPF. "Oh, yeah," he said. "They've pretty much taught me everything I know." He smiled to himself.

"Well, looks like Yuri kidnapped the wrong boy, doesn't it?" said John Stalwart, laughing.

Jack really wanted to tell his dad all about the GPF, but he knew he couldn't. He decided it was safer to change the subject. "How are you feeling now? If I can get us to Mission Control, can you stop the launch?"

"I think my head is clearing now," said his dad. "Just get me to the control desk. Even if Yuri has entered the code, there's still time to hit the 'emergency shutdown' button. That's the best way to put an end to the launch."

"Terrific," said Jack. He looked at the time on his Watch Phone. It was 7:10 A.M. There were only twenty minutes left until the rocket took off.

Given the time it took Vigo to drive here, Jack reckoned they were at least five miles away from Mission Control. There was no way they could run—even the fastest runner in the world couldn't sprint it in twenty minutes. There was only one thing to do.

Reaching into his Book Bag, Jack pulled his Flyboard out. He snapped it together and laid it on the ground.

"Hop on!" said Jack to his dad, motioning for him to climb on top.

"What kind of skateboard is this?" asked his dad. Jack could tell he was confused by the fact that it didn't have wheels.

"I borrowed it from Richard," said Jack, trying to act cool. "His dad picked it up in Hong Kong while he was there on business. It's not in the shops at home yet," he added. Jack thought it best not to say anything else.

"Impressive," said his dad, stepping on. "It's amazing what toys kids have now."

"Yeah, this is a really special one. And now put this on," Jack said as he tossed a rubbery shell to his dad.

As Jack's father placed the Noggin Mold on his head, it hardened into a helmet. The Noggin Mould was great protection when you were climbing, skiing or just going fast.

Jack took the spare Noggin Mold from his Book Bag and placed it on his own

head. When he was ready, he stepped
onto the Flyboard in front of his dad, and
his dad grabbed hold of his shoulders.

Without his father seeing, Jack tapped a
few commands into his Watch Phone. The
Flyboard gently lifted and two hydrogen
jets popped out from underneath. Within
moments, the Stalwarts were sailing away
from the rocket and toward Mission
Control.

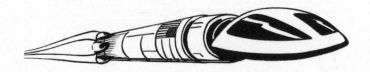

Chapter 12:
The Arrival

Once they were near the main building,
Jack began to slow the Flyboard down.
He turned to his dad. "Is there a back
entrance to this place?" he asked.

His dad pointed to the left of the
building. "On that side of the building is
the delivery area," he said into Jack's ear.
"Nobody will be in there now."

Slowly guiding the Flyboard to the left,
Jack quieted the hydrogen jets down to a

hum. He and his dad hopped off. Once the jets disappeared, Jack packed the Flyboard away.

"I hope Richard has insurance for that thing," said his dad. He was obviously impressed with how the Flyboard worked.

"I'll tell him," said Jack, who was already thinking about the next part of his plan.

"How do we get in?" he asked.

"Thumbprint identification," said his dad. He walked over and placed his thumb on a black box outside the door. "Let's hope Yuri hasn't flagged me," he said.

Jack knew there was a risk that Yuri had blocked his dad's access to Mission Control. Thankfully, he hadn't, because the door to the delivery area opened immediately.

"I guess Yuri thought we were toast," said Jack's dad with a grin.

As they entered the room, Jack and his dad quickly crouched down low. His father was right about it being a delivery area, but wrong about the fact that nobody would be at work.

Jack counted at least five men, two

driving forklifts and three on the floor.
Across the room, he spied a door with a
sign above it saying, THIS WAY TO MISSION
CONTROL ROOM.

Jack nodded to his dad that he would
go first. He hunched over and ran to a
nearby stack of boxes, then waited a few
seconds before calling his dad over. When
he made it, Jack sighed in relief. And so it
went on, until the two Stalwarts reached
the opposite door.

Jack's dad placed his thumb on another black thumbprint box. The door opened, and the pair dashed from the delivery area into a long hallway.

"Where to next?" asked Jack. His dad knew the place better than almost anyone.

"This way," said his dad, pointing down the hallway toward another door.

When they got to it, they pushed it open and stepped through.

Chapter 13:
The Surprise

Thankfully, there was so much going on in the room that when the Stalwarts entered, nobody seemed to notice. They scurried around the back and found a corner hidden from sight.

Jack glanced at his Watch Phone. It was ten minutes until the launch. He took out his Google Goggles, set them to "maximum length" and furtively glanced around for Yuri.

Jack's dad looked at him. "Are those from Hong Kong too?" he asked.

"No," whispered Jack. "I got them from a shop selling toy spy gadgets. But they work really well."

As Jack scanned the room, he noticed a large glass viewing box on the first floor. Yuri was standing inside watching over Mission Control. A man came in and greeted Yuri. Jack grabbed his Ear Amp from his Book Bag and quickly plunged it

into his ear. He tapped on it twice to increase its hearing distance. Listening carefully, Jack tried to make out what they were saying.

"We're almost there," said Yuri. "Without you, we wouldn't have the code."

"No problem, boss," said the other man. "It's been my pleasure to serve you."

Jack guessed the other man was Alexei, the hacker.

As Jack watched Yuri, he saw him walk to a microphone mounted on a desk. Yuri flipped a switch, and then began to speak.

"Team!" he said. "In ten minutes, we will make history! Everybody take your positions."

The Ear Amp was so sensitive to noise that the sound of Yuri's voice roared into Jack's ears. Shaking and smacking his head sideways, Jack forced the Ear Amp to fall out.

Jack and his dad watched as the workers did as they were told. They walked to their stations and prepared for liftoff.

"I need to get to the control panel," said Jack's dad. "There might be a way to lock the keypad and stop Yuri from entering the code."

"Okay," said Jack. "I'll keep a close eye on Yuri." But before he let his dad go, he tried to give him some advice. "Try to keep low," he whispered to him. "We don't want anyone to know we're here."

Jack's father nodded in agreement, and then scurried to a desk across from the control panel. He crouched down just beside it, and when the woman who was working at it walked away, he made his way over to the panel itself.

When Jack saw his dad touching some buttons, he figured he was disabling the keypad as planned. Jack was finally starting to relax.

But just when things were going their way, Jack heard a loud scream from the front of the room. It was Vigo, and he was carrying what looked like a Super Soaker.

Before Jack could do anything, Vigo lifted it up and pointed it in the direction of his dad. He'd been spotted! A powerful light burst out of the front and into Jack's dad, throwing him backward. His father crashed through some computer monitors and fell hard onto the carpeted floor.

Vigo ran toward Jack's father as everyone in the control room screamed and ducked for cover. The Russian roughly grabbed John Stalwart and began to cart him away. Jack looked at Yuri, who was watching everything from above. Leaning close to the microphone again, Yuri made another announcement.

"Don't worry, ladies and gentlemen," he said. "As I told you, John Stalwart has gone a bit mad. We are taking him back to the hospital now. The light that you saw," he added, "has merely stunned him. He'll be all right in a few minutes."

People looked around at one another nervously. "Please, everybody," said Yuri, "get back to work. Don't forget, we have to make John proud and launch his rocket."

Jack was really fuming now. Yuri was using his dad's name to cheer these people on into launching the rocket! Jack knew his dad was only stunned, but it didn't matter. Anyone who hurt a member of the Stalwart family was going to regret it. Jack would make sure of that.

Chapter 14:
The Only One

Jack watched Vigo as he carried his dad to the glass box upstairs and strapped him to a chair for the second time. They clearly had no intention of taking him to a hospital. Jack guessed Yuri wanted to keep a closer eye on his father, but at least he wasn't looking for Jack.

Glancing at his Watch Phone, Jack felt a slight twinge of panic. There were only five minutes left until Yuri would try to enter the code.

Jack thought through his options. He could call the Russian police, but Mars Mission Control was miles from anywhere. If he called them, they would probably be too late.

He could summon the security guards on site, but Jack wasn't sure whether they could be trusted. After all, Yuri was a powerful man, and Jack didn't know how many others Yuri had working for him on his sinister plans.

Another option was to rescue his dad and get him to try and block the keypad again. But that would take time—time that Jack didn't have.

The only person Jack could count on was himself. And the only way to stop the launch was to let Yuri enter the code. Only when the countdown started could Jack press the EMERGENCY SHUTDOWN button. As his dad said, it was the final way to completely stop the rocket launch. But he still needed to get to the control panel without being seen. Jack sat back in the corner and started thinking of a new plan.

Chapter 15:
The Cat's Attack

For some reason, Jack started to think about his GPF instructor Mr. Dee's survival class. In it, he taught recruits to think and act like animals when it came to attack. Jack liked to pretend to be a cat. He could lie in wait, and then pounce on someone when he was least expected.

This thought gave him an idea about how to stop Yuri and the Mars mission launch. He looked around. Next to him was a steel column that rose to a beam near the ceiling.

"Perfect," he said to himself.

Opening the sole on his left shoe, Jack took out two blue pellets. These were the GPF's Smoke-Screen Pellets. He then took two sheets of Sticky Treads and placed the sheets on the bottom of his shoes.

With his hands free, he reached into his Book Bag for his KlimbKit and clipped it to his belt. Then he grabbed his Gripper Gloves and slipped one onto each hand.

Jack placed his hands around the steel column nearby and, using the Sticky Treads and the grip of his gloves, he climbed to the top. By the time he got

there, his arms and legs were aching, but from that position he could see the whole of Mars Mission Control. It was perfect for his plan.

It was 7:26 A.M., and Yuri and Alexei were leaving the glass box and walking downstairs. Jack looked over to his dad, who was finally coming around. He tried to signal to him, but unfortunately, his dad didn't see him.

As Yuri and Alexei reached the control panel, the clock flicked over to 7:27 A.M. It was only three minutes until liftoff.

Looking around the room, Jack couldn't find Vigo anywhere. After he'd tied up John Stalwart, he'd left the glass box and was nowhere to be seen.

Jack watched the time tick down. When it reached thirty seconds to countdown, he opened his KlimbKit. Positioning it where he wanted it to go, Jack pushed the EJECT button. A thin but strong string shot out from inside and wrapped itself around one of the rafters. He tugged on it, making sure it was secure.

After Yuri punched in the code, a woman's voice came over the loud speaker: *"Mission launch has been activated."*

The crowd of workers clapped and cheered.

Now was Jack's only chance. He had to activate the emergency button before the countdown reached zero. Leaping from the beam, Jack swung through Mission Control like Spiderman.

Aiming for the control desk, he let himself fall, landing on Yuri and Alexei and knocking them down.

"Owww!" yelled Yuri as he crumpled under Jack's weight.

"Urggh!" groaned Alexei, who'd been thrown on his side.

"Rocket to lift off in ten . . . nine . . ."

There was no time to waste. Jack stepped over Yuri's face and made his way toward the control desk. He spied the EMERGENCY SHUTDOWN button and put his hand out. But just as he was about to push it, something came flying at him from the side.

Alexei ploughed into Jack, throwing him onto the floor.

"Eight . . . seven . . ."

Jack could hear the rocket boosters roar over the loud speaker. The Mars spacecraft was about to take off.

Yuri and Alexei gathered together in front of the desk. They were blocking Jack from going anywhere near the emergency button.

"Go ahead and try that again!" shouted Yuri.

"Six . . . five . . ."

"Come on!" yelled Yuri, wanting Jack to strike.

"Two against one sounds pretty fair!" squealed Alexei.

"Four . . . three . . ."

Jack was breathing heavily now. There were only two seconds left. He reached into his trouser pocket and pulled out his Smoke-Screen Pellets, then threw one at Yuri's cheek and the other toward Alexei's

nose. As soon as they hit, the pellets
stuck and burst open, releasing a dark
blue smoke in front of their eyes. Yuri and
Alexei couldn't see a thing.

The Russians frantically shook their
heads, trying to get the pellets off. But
GPF Smoke-Screen Pellets don't come off
easily, at least not until after two minutes.

Jack ran around the blinded men and clambered onto the desk. The men's hands were swooping wildly in an attempt to catch him.

"*Two . . .*"

Within that second, Jack saw the button again. He pushed it as quickly as he could.

Just then, a horrible noise blared through Mission Control. Jack wondered if the rocket was blasting off.

BEEP!

BEEP!

BEEP!

The computerized voice came over the speaker again.

"*Emergency shutdown has been activated. Liftoff has been canceled.*"

It took a few seconds to register, but Jack had done it. He'd stopped the rocket from taking off!

"Noooo!" yelled a familiar voice. It was Vigo. The third Russian had come back.

FLASH!

A burst of light went off.

FLASH!

And then another.

Vigo was zapping anything in sight with the light gun. Jack crouched down out of the way. People were fleeing everywhere. He saw Vigo running toward Yuri and Alexei, who were still struggling to see through the thick blue smoke.

As the three Russians stood together, Jack smiled. He pulled his Net Tosser out of his Book Bag and threw it in the direction of the men, where it broke open and cast a net over the thugs.

Vigo pulled the trigger on his gun, but the burst of light bounced back at them from the Net Tosser's bulletproof walls.

"Owww!" screeched Yuri as the heat of the light burned off one of his eyebrows.

At that moment, the doors at the back of Mission Control were flung open and a team of Russian police stormed through. Jack was confused. He hadn't called anyone yet.

"You're not the only one with clever ideas," said a voice from behind him. Jack turned around. It was his dad.

"Dad!" said Jack, completely stunned. The last time he'd seen his dad, he was tied to a chair. "But how did you escape?" he asked.

"I was able to free myself by hopping over to some scissors on Yuri's desk," Jack's dad replied.

Jack was totally impressed. It must have been his dad who'd called the cops. In the end, they hadn't taken that long to arrive. Jack threw his arms around his father and gave him a hug.

"I'm proud of you, son," John Stalwart said. "Without you, the rocket would have gone into space,

and those astronauts might have died."
He let out a big sigh. "We'll have to phone
your mum—she must be worried sick. I'll
make a call and book you on the next
flight out of Moscow. It's time we got you
home."

Chapter 16:
The Mind Game

While they were talking, Jack made a few taps on his wrist. The Net Tosser released its grip, and the cops swarmed over to the men. They cuffed Yuri, Alexei and Vigo and hauled them away.

All in all, Jack thought, things couldn't have turned out better. But it was about that time in every mission when Jack had to find a secret way home.

"Dad," he said, "can I see you over

here?" He led his dad over to a quiet corner of the room.

"I thought you'd appreciate this," he said, giving him a box that he'd pulled from his Book Bag. "It's another one of Richard's latest toys."

"Okay," said his dad, taking the box in his hand.

"Now, look into the middle," said Jack, "and tell me what you see."

"All I can see is something swirling inside," he replied.

"Perfect," said Jack. "Keep looking at it. This really is an amazing gadget. I promise."

Jack's dad was slowly being transfixed by the GPF's Mind Eraser. It was the most powerful tool for erasing somebody's short-term memory. Although he hated doing it, Jack couldn't let his dad remember he was there. The only other people who knew about Jack were the three Russians, and no one would believe those criminals.

With his dad distracted, Jack slipped out unnoticed through the back door. Outside, he could see Yuri, Alexei and Vigo being thrown into the back of a Russian police van. When the doors to the van slammed shut, Jack moved around the building to a quiet space.

He pulled out his foldaway map and opened it onto the ground. Then he touched the outline of England and waited for the light inside to fire up.

When it did, he yelled, "Off to England!" The map swallowed him whole and sent him back to the New Forest.

Chapter 17:
The Return to Earth

When Jack arrived, he found himself in
the exact spot from where he'd left. He
tucked his portable Magic Map into his
Book Bag, and tapped his Watch Phone
for the latest GPF news. He hit the video
button so he could see a live report.

Evelyn Lewis, chief reporter for the GPF,
was there in Moscow's Red Square.

*"Yuri Ivanov, the commander of the
Mars Mission Team, was arrested in*

Russia today on a number of charges, including kidnapping, command of a deadly light weapon and knowingly trying to send astronauts into space in an unsafe spacecraft. Vigo Popov and Alexei Smirnov were also arrested. Secret Agent 'Courage' assisted in the capture and arrest of all three men.

"As a consequence of Mr. Ivanov's criminal behavior, John Stalwart was named the new commander of the Mars Mission Team.

" 'I'm proud to serve this team as their new commander," said Mr. Stalwart. 'Once we've added the appropriate safeguards to the craft,' he added, 'we plan to send the first man to Mars.'

"When asked who assisted in the capture of Yuri Ivanov, Mr. Stalwart shook his head and admitted, 'It's strange, but I really can't remember what happened.'"

Jack logged out of his Watch Phone and headed back to where Richard and Charlie were lying. He sat down beside his friends and took a few moments to think about the mission.

Not only had he nabbed three bad guys, he'd saved the astronauts and helped his dad land his dream job. And he'd done it all without his father remembering a thing. For now, Jack's secret was safe from his family.

"So, did you survive?" asked Richard.

Jack froze. How did he know? Did someone see something?

"You know, your trip to the restroom?" Richard continued.

Jack breathed a sigh of relief. "Barely," he said, trying to be funny. "Almost flushed myself down the toilet."

At that the three friends started to howl with laughter. It was funny, Jack thought—friends always had a habit of bringing each other down to earth.

The Quest for
Aztec Gold:
MEXICO

BOOK ⑩

Read the first
chapter here

Chapter 1:
The Chase

Secret Agent Jack Stalwart was running for his life. He was sprinting across an open plain, trying to escape from four dark shadows that were chasing him at top speed.

Jack spied a prickly bush up ahead. Rather than run around it, he jumped right over.

BLAM!

His feet crashed to the ground, spraying sandy dust into the air.

BLAM! BLAM! BLAM! BLAM!

The shadows jumped too, grunting as they landed. It felt as though they were close enough to almost touch Jack. But he was still a few seconds ahead.

Reaching for his Book Bag, he tried to grab one of his life-saving gadgets. But Jack's Book Bag wasn't on his back. Strange, he thought. It was always there.

Out of nowhere, Jack stumbled. He fell forward, his hands slamming into the sand. He rolled over several times and tried to get himself upright. But the shadows soon reached him, howling with evil laughter.

"Noooo!" Jack screamed, as the dark figures leaned over and . . .